**www.mascotbooks.com**

**For more information, please contact:**
Mascot Books
P.O. Box 220157
Chantilly, VA 20153-0157
info@mascotbooks.com

CPSIA Code: PRT0911A
ISBN: 1-936319-79-9
ISBN-13: 978-1-936319-79-4

Printed in the United States

"This book is dedicated to my husband, John Kaminsky"

~ Denise L. Kaminsky

2

On a beautiful fall morning, Nittany Lion went for a hike on Mount Nittany. Central Pennsylvania was beautiful this time of the year. "The Penn State football game this afternoon will be great," said Nittany Lion to himself.

Looking over to the creek, Nittany Lion spotted Turtle climbing out of the trickling stream. "Hello, Turtle," said Nittany Lion.

Before Turtle could answer he heard, **"HICCUP, HICCUP!"**

"Uh oh," said Nittany Lion. **"HICCUP,"** he said again. "I can't go to the game with hiccups. **HICCUP."**

Turtle said, "I know the cure. Just drink some water." Nittany Lion drank some water from his water bottle. He waited. Then...

**"HICCUP, HICCUP.** Oh no, oh no, it didn't work. **HICCUP,** thanks for trying to help," said Nittany Lion.

"Don't give up," said Turtle.

Nittany Lion hiked on and soon spotted Blue Jay. **"HICCUP,"** said Nittany Lion instead of Hello.

"Oh, Nittany Lion. You have those darn hiccups," said Blue Jay.

"Yes, **HICCUP,"** he said. "I can help," said Blue Jay. "Close your eyes, please."

**"SQUA-A-A-W-K!"**
called Blue Jay. Nittany Lion jumped.
"Why did you do that?" Blue Jay said,
"I was trying to scare away your hiccups."

**"HICCUP,"** said Nittany Lion. "Oh no,
again it didn't work."

**"HICCUP,** thanks for trying to help,"
said Nittany Lion.

"Don't give up," said Blue Jay.

Nittany Lion hiked on and soon he met Squirrel sitting on a branch eating an acorn. "Hello, Squirrel, **HICCUP,**" said Nittany Lion.

"Hello, Nittany Lion. Did I hear you hiccup?" asked Squirrel.

"Yes, **HICCUP,**" Nittany Lion answered. Squirrel asked, "Do you hate hiccups just as much as I do?"

"Yes, **HICCUP,**" Nittany lion said.

"I have just the cure for you. Please stand under my branch," requested Squirrel. Nittany Lion moved over to where Squirrel pointed.

Squirrel lowered his tail and began to tickle Nittany Lion behind his ear.

Nittany Lion laughed and laughed and ...
**HICCUPPED** and **HICCUPPED.**
"Oh, they won't go away. Oh, they won't go away."

"Sorry, Nittany Lion, I thought tickling you with my tail would get rid of your hiccups.

**"HICCUP,** and thanks for trying to help," said Nittany Lion.

"Don't give up" said Squirrel.

Nittany Lion walked on and soon came to a cave. **"HICCUP,** hello. Grandmother Bear are you home? **"HICCUP,"** he called.

Grandmother Bear lumbered out. "Good morning, Nittany Lion. Out for a hike?"

"Yes, **HICCUP.** But I got the... **HICCUPS,"** he answered. "Can you help me?"

"I know just the cure. It is quite simple," Grandmother Bear said. "Just do as I say. Start drinking from your water bottle while I press on your ears. When I let go, stop drinking and count slowly and silently to thirty. Your hiccups will be gone."

"Okay, **HICCUP,**" said Nittany Lion. He did exactly as Grandmother Bear said.

Nittany Lion listened, then smiled and softly said, "It worked!" All they heard was the chirping of the birds.

"Oh thank you, Grandmother Bear. It worked. Now I can go to the Penn State football game this afternoon and cheer like crazy," said Nittany Lion.

"You're welcome," said Grandmother Bear. "Go Penn State!"

Nittany Lion hiked down Mount Nittany just in time for the Penn State game.


**Note:** Grandma Bear's cure really does work.

# THE END.